Table of Contents

Chapter 1

The Toy Shop

The little boy was very excited because today he was going on adventures with his mother. They were going shopping and he was very excited because there would be so many interesting things to see. He knew he would get to go to the toy shop. He loved to look at all the toys in the window.

By the time they both put their coats on and took the bus to town the little boy could wait no longer. "Mummy, please, may I go and look in the toy shop, please? PLEASE?"

The little boy's mother smiled fondly. "Yes you may!" she said. "You know where it is. Off you go."

The little boy ran all the way to the toyshop. When he reached it, he couldn't believe his eyes. He didn't know where to look first!

There in the back of the window was a huge brightly coloured beach ball and some brave looking soldiers with bright red coats. Off to one side there was an ambulance with a big red cross and a bright red light on top. At the front he saw a large yellow transport truck. It was all very exciting! The little boy forgot all about them when he saw the teddy bear. It was golden brown and fluffy. Quite the best teddy bear he had ever seen, with big soft ears, a smiling little mouth, and bright, sparkling eyes. The Teddy Bear winked at him and the little boy was startled. He didn't know how, but he was sure that the teddy bear could see everything that was happening in the street.

"Please, please may I have that teddy bear," he begged his mother as she came out of the butcher's shop. "It's the sweetest, most lovely, bear that I've ever seen!"

"Well" said Mummy, "It's almost Christmas, maybe Santa will bring you a teddy bear."

Every night until Christmas the little boy

wished and wished. Every night as he said his prayers he asked for Santa to bring him that very teddy bear. Then he would cross the fingers of each hand and go to sleep. It had to be that bear. No other bear would do. He just knew that bear was magic!

Chapter 2

Christmas

On Christmas morning the little boy woke up very early. The house was totally silent. Mummy and daddy were still asleep but he couldn't wait any longer. This was the very day for which he had been waiting so very patiently.

Moving quietly, he put on his dressing gown and tiptoed down the stairs. Under the Christmas tree were a lot of parcels. Some he recognized right away. They came from Grandma and Grandpa and his Aunties and Uncles but he was looking for a parcel that came from Santa.

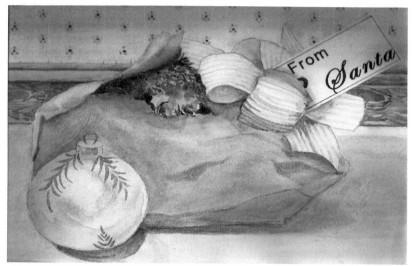

There it was! It was just what he was looking for: a big parcel and it said "From Santa." He squeezed it. Yes! It was soft. He tore a small corner of the paper and a fluffy foot popped out. The little boy gazed at it. He was so happy that he jumped up and down. He was very careful to jump quietly because Mummy and Daddy were still fast asleep.

He grabbed the parcel and quickly tore off the rest of the paper. Oh yes! It was the very same teddy bear. Then as he sat and watched a very strange thing happened. The teddy bear sat up!

"Oh thank you" said the teddy bear "It was very stuffy in there." He raised his arms above his head, stretched, and gave his ears a wiggle. He bounced to his feet and ran to the centre of the room. "My name is Edward Bear," said the teddy bear. "I think we're going to have a lot of fun together. Do you believe in magic?"

"I think so but I'm not sure. Will you tell me what you know about magic?" asked the little boy.

"Oh it's very simple and yet a little complicated at the same time!" said the bear. "What you have to do is believe in love, be as nice and kind as you are able, and laugh and sing and dance. Then, you may become aware of all kinds of magical happenings."

"I think I can do that," the little boy said.

"It can be a bit tricky sometimes," said Edward. "However, if you are watching carefully, you may be surprised at some of the things that occur. Some of the most magical times happen when you are having fun."

"Oh hooray! Let us begin right away," said the boy.

The boy and the bear ran to the window, jumped up on the bench and looked out together. "Is that snow?" asked Edward. "I've heard all about snow. It sounds like a lot of fun."

"Yes it is," said the little boy. "Snow is kind of like a riddle. It can be soft and yet hard at the same time! Can you imagine that? It is very cold and when it goes down your neck, it feels yucky. It will make your mittens all wet but you can build the grandest things from it! You can make castles and forts and slides. Really, you can make anything that you are able to imagine."

"That sounds like magic to me!" said the bear. "May we go out and play in it? Will your Mummy and Daddy let us?"

Edward was so excited. The little boy took his hand and they danced round and round and round the room singing. "We love snow. We love snow. We love SNOW."

While they were dancing, they heard footsteps on the floor above. "Ssshhh!" said Edward, "somebody is coming."

"It's only my Daddy," said the little boy.
Edward flopped down towards the floor. "Nobody must know that I'm magic," whispered Edward into the boy's ear. "If any grown-ups find out, I'll lose my magic powers." Then he fell back onto the floor and lay still.

"To whom are you talking?" asked the little boy's father as he came into the room.

"My teddy bear," said the little boy as he scooped up Edward and hugged him tightly.

Chapter 3

Playing in the snow

After breakfast the little boy put on his snowsuit and his hat and mittens. His mother opened the door to let him go out and play in the back garden.

The boy carried Edward to that part of the garden that was hidden behind the garage and couldn't be seen from the house. As soon as they were around the corner, Edward jumped down onto the snow. They ran around, fell into the snow, made angels and snowballs and had lots of fun. They laughed and giggled, and played and played.

When they went back indoors, Edward's fur was all very wet and he was very cold. The little boy took him into his room and rubbed him down with a big fluffy towel. "That tickles!" Edward chuckled. The little boy giggled and rubbed him more and more because Edward had such a funny belly laugh. The boy loved Edward's big belly laugh! It gave the boy a bubbly feeling around his heart. "Well," said Edward when he was warm and dry again. "I can see I will have to get myself some clothes."

"Teddy bears don't wear clothes," said the little boy seriously.

"Well, I am certainly not an ordinary teddy bear. I'm Edward Bear and when I get some clothes, I shall be Edward Covered."

The little boy thought about this for a while and decided that Edward was quite right. He ran downstairs right then to ask his mother what she could do about getting some clothes for Edward.

She was in the kitchen very busy making Christmas dinner. The room was filled with yummy smells and Mummy was stirring and mixing and chopping.

"Edward got very cold and wet when we were playing in the snow and we think he should have some clothes. Can you get him some, Mummy please?

"Why did you choose to call him Edward?" asked the little boy's mother.

"Well, he is a very proper little bear," said the little boy. "Teddy is much too informal."

The little boy's mother and father laughed at the boy and his mother said kindly, "After dinner I will look in the attic and see if I can find something nice for Edward to wear."

"Oh thank you Mummy," said the little boy as he ran upstairs to tell Edward the good news.

Chapter 4

Edward Covered

Everybody was very full after their huge Christmas dinner. The little boy's father went upstairs to have a nap after he and Mummy had finished the dishes.

"Okay! I'm ready," said Mummy, "Lets go up to the attic and see what we can find." Edward was so excited he could hardly keep from talking out loud so he snuggled in close to the little boy and whispered, "goody, goody, and GOODY!" The little boy gave him a secret little hug.

They all trooped up the dusty attic stairs. Mummy went to the big trunk and started looking through it. First she pulled out a pair of fancy pink woolly pants. Edward wrinkled his nose and was very relieved when they were too small.

Next, she brought out a small pair of forest green velvet trouser. Edward smiled a great big smile as the little boy put the pants on him. The little boy's Mother picked Edward up and looked at him. "The pants are too long for his little legs, but we can soon fix that," she said as she rolled up the trouser legs. "I will turn the legs up and sew them for you later." She then turned back to the trunk and once again searched through it for more clothing.

"Here you go," said Mummy as she pulled out a little tartan shirt out of the trunk.

"All we need now is a pair of shoes," said the little boy.

"I think I have just the thing," said Mummy as she pulled a pair of white leather shoes out of a small box beside the trunk. "These look just the right size," she said with a smile. "They were yours when you were a baby."

"Oh thank you Mummy!" said the little boy and gave her a great big hug.

Edward wanted to say thank you as well, but he couldn't. Grownups were not allowed to know that he could talk. He smiled his biggest, brightest smile instead and hoped that the little boy's mother would understand.

Page 25

Afterwards in the little boy's room, Edward paraded up and down and looked in the mirror. "I'm so happy," he sang. "I have lovely shoes, beautiful clothes and the very best friend a bear could have!"

"This has been such a wonderful day," said Edward Covered. "We have had so much fun. I wonder what will happen tomorrow? There are so many things I want to learn."

"We can learn things together and have a lot of fun at the same time," said the little boy.

"Yes," said Edward. "We can have a lot of adventures together and that is the very best way to learn new and exciting things."

"Today has been a grand adventure for me" said the little boy. "I have learned something important already. I've learned a quite a lot about magic."

"Part of magic is believing something, even if you can't quite prove it," said Edward.

"I can do that!" said the boy.

Then the little boy and the teddy bear called Edward Covered held hands and danced in a circle. They thought about all the adventures they would have in the days to come and they both smiled gigantic smiles.

Edward Covered

The adventures of a small boy
and his teddy bear

THE END

About the author

Margaret M. Sinclair

1924 - 2013
Margaret conceived the stories of Edward
Covered more than sixty years ago.

About the illustrator

Sharon Ramsay Curtis
Artist at The Artful Garden Gallery,
Painter,
Teacher,
Potter,
Raconteur,
and
Generally Interesting Person.
Sharon lives in Colborne, Ontario, Canada

Dedication
For Max and Bella and all the "grands" who may
follow. With deepest love!
Granny Sharon

Made in the USA
Charleston, SC
11 August 2014